CLARENCE
The Cranberry Who Couldn't Bounce

This book is dedicated

to all children

who can see God's handiwork

in the natural world.

Published by Harvest Home Books
Post Office Box 1181
East Dennis, Massachusetts 02641

Copyright © 2002 by Jim Coogan

ISBN 0-9672596-3-0

Cover design and page layout by Jackie Rockwell of Rockwell Design, West Yarmouth, Massachusetts.

Printed in the United States of America.

Additional copies of *Clarence the Cranberry Who Couldn't Bounce*, or the author's previous books – *Cape Cod Companion* and *Cape Cod Voyage* – may be obtained by contacting Harvest Home Books.

CLARENCE
The Cranberry Who Couldn't Bounce

Story and Illustrations by

Jim Coogan

Harvest Home Books

The peeper frogs had finished their spring song. The days
were long and sunny. It was summer in the cranberry bog.

The pretty cranberry blossoms were visited by busy little bees. By midsummer, the small green berries were formed.

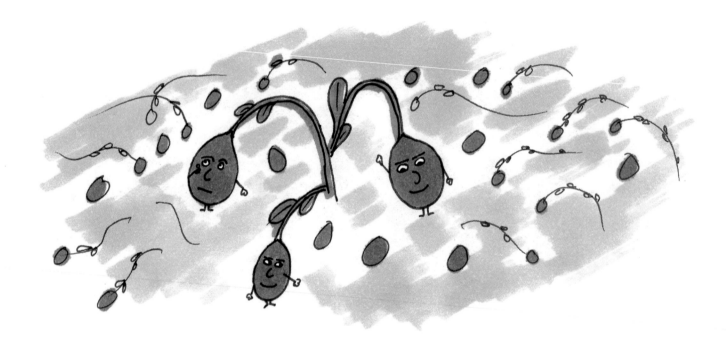

One of these berries was Clarence!

And there were millions of his relatives.

Clarence had many famous ancestors.

1620

Cranberries greeted the Pilgrims.

And were very revolutionary!

Some even went on long ocean voyages.

As he hung from his vine in the
sun, Clarence grew large and strong.

He obeyed his mother and father and followed
all the rules that good cranberries should.

He *never* got too hot.

He drank *lots* of water.

And he made sure that worms stayed away from him.

In fact, Clarence was a perfect cranberry in all ways except one . . .

WHUMP!

Clarence could not bounce!

He tried everything he could think of because he knew that cranberries have to bounce to be perfect. But, despite his best efforts, it was still . . . **WHUMP!**

A perfect cranberry has to bounce through the sorting machine at harvest time. Berries that didn't bounce were not taken.

He watched his friends and relatives as they practiced
bouncing all around him.

Clarence was getting desperate!

It was starting to look hopeless.

WHUMP!

16

He felt so embarrassed that he began to turn *red*!

Clarence was so busy worrying
about his bouncing that he never even
noticed that all the other cranberries
were also turning red.

He thought that he must be
too heavy to bounce.

So he went on a diet . . .

... And he began to exercise.

The cooler nights were a sign that autumn was near.
The cranberry bog was flooded and Clarence felt a great
noise coming toward him . . .

Clarence held his breath as the noise came closer.

Suddenly he was thrown from side to side and he lost his grip on the vine.

And just like a cork he popped to the surface of the water.

It was *very, very* scary!

From the flooded bog he was shoveled up a ramp into a big truck.

After a long ride he was dumped into a sorting chute at the cranberry packing plant.

Clarence found himself heading toward the sorting machine.

He was lifted higher and higher and then dumped into the sorting machine.

Inside the machine it was very dark.

And he felt himself FALLING . . .

DOWN

HE

WENT

It wasn't exactly a ping . . .
But it wasn't a
WHUMP! either.

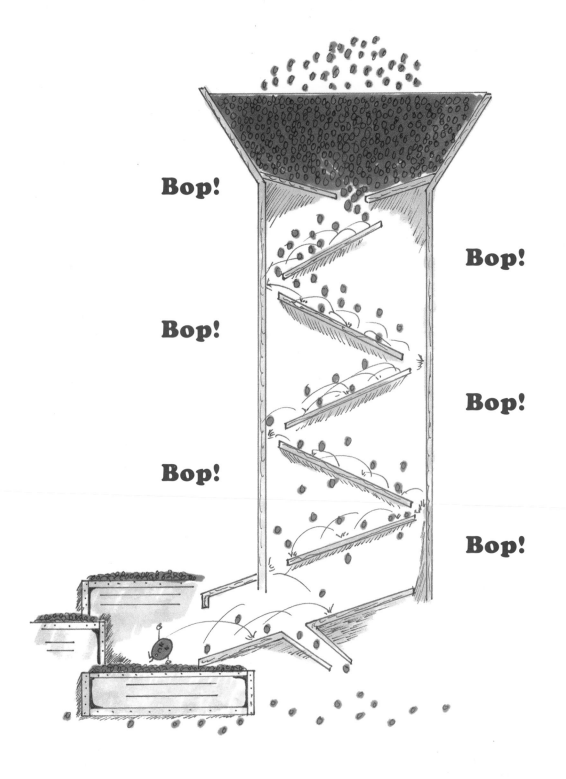

Bop!

Bop!

Bop!

Bop!

Bop!

Bop!

28

He rested in the box and sighed with relief.

When it counted he had made it.

But just when he was beginning to relax and feel successful,
Clarence felt himself being lifted out of the box.

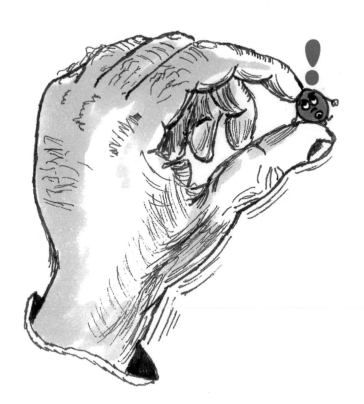

CRANBERRIES

Clarence heard a loud voice shout,
"Hey Fred, here's another one!"
He was placed in a large bowl
with other cranberries.
He was sure the
men thought he
really hadn't
bounced on
his own.

The men
took the
bowl out
of the sorting
room and away
from the packing plant.

Clarence was miserable!

But Clarence soon learned that he shouldn't have worried. He had been chosen, along with the other berries in the bowl, as the finest of the harvest. He was the star of the grand display at the Cranberry Festival.

If you look very carefully, you can see him.
Can you find Clarence?